Fireflies, Peach Pies & Lullabies

story by Virginia Kroll • *pictures by* Nancy Cote

Simon & Schuster Books for Young Readers

SIMON & SCHUSTER BOOKS FOR YOUNG READERS   An imprint of Simon & Schuster Children's Publishing Division   1230 Avenue of the Americas   New York, NY 10020   Text copyright © 1995 by Virginia Kroll Illustrations copyright © 1995 by Nancy Cote   All rights reserved, including the right of reproduction in whole or in part in any form   SIMON & SCHUSTER BOOKS FOR YOUNG READERS is a trademark of Simon & Schuster. Designed by Christy Hale   The text of this book is set in Bruce Old Style. The illustrations are rendered in gouache. Printed in Hong Kong by South China Printing Co. (1988) Ltd.   10   9   8   7   6   5   4   3   2   1   *Library of Congress Cataloging-in-Publication Data* Kroll, Virginia L.   Fireflies, peach pies, and lullabies / story by Virginia Kroll ; pictures by Nancy Cote.   p.   cm.   Summary : When Francie's Great-Granny Annabel dies of Alzheimer's disease, Francie finds a way to help people remember the real person rather than the shell she had become as the disease ran its course. ISBN 0-689-80291-9   [1. Death—Fiction.   2. Memory—Fiction.   3. Alzheimer's disease—Fiction.]   I. Cote, Nancy, ill.   II.Title. PZ7.K9227Fi   1995   [E]—dc20   94-19373

For Father John R. Aurelio, with love
—V. K.

To mothers and grandmothers everywhere
who light the fireflies in their children's eyes.
This one's for you, Mom, love
—N. C.

FRANCIE kept her eyes on her cereal and her ears on Mama and Aunt Patrice. They were talking about Great-Granny Annabel again.

"It's like she's nothing but an empty shell nowadays."

That made Francie think of peanuts at the circus and walnuts at Thanksgiving.

Francie's great-granny Annabel forgot how to get dressed, and she called her family by the wrong names. Most of the time, she didn't talk at all, but just sat staring at something no one else could see. And sometimes she'd say, "Uh-huh, yes siree," as if someone had asked her a question.

Great-Granny Annabel was soft and warm when Francie leaned up against her. On good days, she even put her hand on Francie's head and twirled a finger around her curls. She wasn't a hard, empty shell. Uh-uh, no siree. No way.

"Know what the worst part is?" Aunt Patrice went on. "Worst part is, this is how everyone will remember her."

"Yes," agreed Mama. "All the good thoughts gone, like an ocean wave just whooshed in and washed all the memories away. Just like that." Mama snapped her fingers.

Francie sipped the milk from her bowl and crept away, leaving Mama and Aunt Patrice to their coffee and their nonsense.

During the week, an ambulance took Great-Granny Annabel to the hospital. Two days later, she died. Francie cried and beat her pillow. She flung Eddy Teddy to the floor, then swooped him up and hugged him fiercely and cried more tears than she thought a pair of eyes could hold. Buckets. Rivers maybe, till she felt empty. That made her think of peanut and walnut shells again, and she got angry. Fist-clenching angry. Foot-stomping mad.

"No-no f-fair," Francie stammered. "I'll remember you different."

Francie took a deep breath and thought she smelled Great-Granny Annabel's cotton-dress smell. She heard the wind chime that Great-Granny Annabel had made from painted wooden spoons. She lay on her bed and rolled up like a caterpillar, snug in the rainbow afghan that Great-Granny Annabel had knitted when Francie got her big-girl bed.

And Francie fell asleep remembering Great-Granny Annabel *different*—dress-smelling, chime-sounding, afghan-snuggling different.

The next afternoon, Francie went to the funeral home with her family. Mama said that Great-Granny Annabel's body was in the long, closed silver coffin up front. Flowers surrounded it, overflowing to the side walls.

People came and said they were sorry. They hugged and cried and went home. Francie watched their eyes and wondered what they saw before, wondered what made their tears flow now. What was making their mouths smile or frown? Were they remembering different, too?

Francie sat on the too-high chairs. She climbed the staircase and stared at the sparkling chandelier till her eyes watered. She watched folks she knew, and strangers, too, sign their names in a black book, and she peeked around a corner to where the funeral-home man was talking to Mama and Aunt Patrice about the services tomorrow.

Suddenly, Francie got an idea.

"Excuse me," she whispered, but nobody heard.

Francie tried to sit still and wait, but her legs wouldn't cooperate. They jumped and jittered. She leaped off her chair and hopscotched across the patterned rug. That made Mama say, "Francie, what?" Finally. At last.

"Do you have some paper and a pen?" Francie asked the funeral-home man.

He opened his desk. "There you go," he said, handing them over.

"That ought to keep you busy," Aunt Patrice said.

Francie returned to the flower-filled room.

She swallowed hard and went to Uncle Louis.

"Could you please write down something special you remember about Great-Granny Annabel?" she asked.

Uncle Louis closed his eyes and sighed. "You bet I can," he answered. "Fireflies. She was the first one ever to take me firefly catching on hot summer nights, down by Cazenovia Creek. We'd hold them in jars just for a while." He took the paper and wrote down his memory, and Francie felt summery-warm.

"That reminds me," Cousin Arthur exclaimed. "I know the name of every bird in this city because of that feeder she kept out back." He took the pen and paper while Francie pictured chickadees and nuthatches nibbling Great-Granny Annabel's sunflower-suet cakes.

Mrs. Keller, Francie's baby-sitter, wrote ANNABEL SAT UP ALL NIGHT WITH ME WHEN MY FATHER HAD HIS ACCIDENT AT WORK.

Mr. Keller's eyes filled with tears. "And remember that poem she wrote me when my own mother passed on?" He took the pen from his wife.

Abraham Hollis, the janitor at St. Barbara's School, said, "She made the most scrumptious peach pies in the country, she did. Picked the peaches herself, too, right off those trees that lean over the church parking lot. Used to bring one by every year, just because I gave her permission. Umm, umm."

And he jotted down PEACH PIES while Francie's mouth watered.

"And don't forget," said his sister, Sarah, "how she donated all those handmade mittens to the giving tree every Christmas."

Francie moved from person to person with her paper and pen.

When Francie got home that night, Mama and Aunt Patrice read the list. They hugged her and cried and added to it in teeny-weeny writing, because it was full, front and back.

Then it was Francie's turn. Familiar tunes were filling her mind. Soft, sweet lullabies that Great-Granny Annabel made up right out of her head. Just like that.

"How do you spell lullabies?" she asked. Mama helped her write it down. Francie put the list under her pillow.

In the morning, she found Father John. He thanked
Francie and touched her cheek. He pulled a pen from his
big black robe and wrote BEST VOICE IN THE CHOIR FOR
THIRTEEN YEARS. Then the list disappeared where the pen
had come from.

When the time came, Father John read the memories one by one. Francie heard a few faint sniffles. Then some loud sighs. And someone chuckled cheerfully. Soon the church was buzzing like a hive full of bees while sweet golden memories spilled over the pews and into the aisles.

Francie studied people's faces. She knew what they saw, what made their eyes glow and their mouths smile.

"How do you like that?" Father John said. "What a celebration of life! Fireflies, peach pies, and lullabies. Amen!"

"Amen!" everyone said over and over. Francie was sure their voices reached right up to heaven.

Then, just for a moment, she thought she heard a tune echoing off the walls. A lullaby. Right from heaven. Uh-huh, yes siree.